Fatal Attraction to Love

Without A Hitch

Book Two

By: Kent HamiIlton

Table of Contents

Chapter One 7

Chapter 2 32

Chapter 3 38

Chapter 4 46

Chapter 5 52

Chapter 6 62

© **Copyright 2020 by : KENT HAMILTON- All rights reserved.**

This document is geared toward providing exact and reliable information in regard to the topic and issue covered. The publication is sold with the idea that the publisher is not required to render accounting, officially permitted, or otherwise, qualified services. If advice is necessary, legal or professional, a practiced individual in the profession should be ordered.

- From a Declaration of Principles which was accepted and approved equally by a Committee of the American Bar Association and a Committee of Publishers and Associations.

In no way is it legal to reproduce, duplicate, or transmit any part of this document in either electronic means or in printed format. Recording of this publication is strictly prohibited and any storage of this document is not allowed unless with written permission from the publisher. All rights reserved.

The information provided herein is stated to be truthful and consistent, in that any liability, in terms of inattention or otherwise, by any usage or abuse of any policies, processes, or directions contained within is the solitary and utter responsibility of the recipient reader. Under no circumstances will any legal responsibility or blame be held against the publisher for any reparation, damages, or monetary loss due to the information herein, either directly or indirectly.

Respective authors own all copyrights not held by the publisher.

The information herein is offered for informational purposes solely, and is universal as so. The presentation of the information is without contract or any type of guarantee assurance.

The trademarks that are used are without any consent, and the publication of the trademark is without permission or backing by the trademark owner. All trademarks and brands within this book are for clarifying purposes only and are the owned by the owners themselves, not affiliated with this document.

Disclaimer:

The information presented in this book represents the views of the publisher as of the date of publication. The publisher reserves the rights to alter update their opinions based on new conditions. This report is for informational purposes only. The author and the publisher do not accept any responsibilities for any liabilities resulting from the use of this information. While every attempt has been made to verify the information provided here, the author and the publisher cannot assume any responsibility for errors, inaccuracies or omissions. Any similarities with people or facts are unintentional

Part II

Chapter One

John woke up to the sound of beeping machines and loud voices. For a moment he forgot where he was.
He looked next to him to make sure the dream that he had just woke up from wasn't real. He dreamt that he was outside Kari's house again. He could see her on the floor through her window. He tried to break the window, but he couldn't. He tried to yell her name, but no words would come out. He felt the fear slowly rise into his chest. The feeling of Kari stroking his hand brought him back to reality.

"Good morning" Kari said with a smile.

She noticed that he had tears in his eyes. He shook his head and told her about the dream. By the time he was done, tears slowly trickled down his cheeks. He couldn't imagine his future without her in it. He knew he wanted her forever. He got up and said he had to run an errand and that she should just rest. He promised her that he would be right back.

He was still moving slow, but he was a man on a mission. He went to the nurses' desk and told them a brief story about he and Kari's whirlwind romance. He asked them to help him with a surprise. They weren't very busy so they jumped into action willingly. Next, John called Mary.

"Good morning, Mary" he said with his voice shaking from excitement.

"Good morning, John. How is Kari?" Mary told him that she was just waking up and would be on her way to the hospital to check on her.

"Perfect, because I need you here to help me with something."

John told her the details of his plan. Mary was excited for her friend. She told him she would be there as soon as she could and agreed to make a stop for him on the way. About two hours later, the plan was all coming together. It was going so effortlessly that John knew it must have been fate. He went back into the room and watched as Kari slept. She looked so peaceful and happy. He gently touched her hand. She woke up and when she saw his face, gave him a look that melted his heart.

"So, how do you like surprises?" John asked as he realized he wasn't sure what her reaction would be.

"I love surprises" she said.

Just then one of the nurses came in the room and said they were going to have to wheel her bed out of the room for a quick test. She assured Kari that everything was just fine with her and the baby. Kari asked John to go with her. John smiled slyly because he knew exactly where they were going. The nurse pushed Kari in her bed down a long hallway. It smelled like bleach and the lights seemed really vivid. The nurse opened a door that said private.

Kari thought it seemed odd, but John was right by her side so she wasn't worried. As they entered the room, Kari saw that Mary was standing there in a beautiful peach sundress and she was holding flowers. Next, she noticed John's friend, Caleb and he was wearing a suit. She was confused. She turned to look at John but he wasn't standing next to her.

He was on his knee and he started to speak:

"Kari Goodbar, I knew I loved you from the day we met. I have never felt so comfortable with anyone. You make me happy when we are together and miserable when we are apart. I don't know how I have survived without you by my side. I can't conceive of my life without you. I can't wait to help you raise the child you're carrying. I will cherish the memories that we have made in such a short time and look forward to new memories in the future as a family. Will you marry me?"

Kari was so shocked, but suddenly it all made sense. She noticed soft music was playing. She saw several of the nurses who had been taking care of her smiling and wiping tears from their eyes. She saw an elderly gray haired man standing by with a bible in his hand. There were bouquets of lilies and roses.

She knew that they had only known each other for such a short period of time. She knew that it was a crazy idea. She knew it was unconventional. She also knew that John was her soul mate. She too couldn't imagine her life without him in it.

She said "Yes, of course I will marry you. I love you so much that my heart aches when we aren't together. I cherish most of the memories that we have" then she laughed lightly. "I can't wait to raise this baby with you. I know that you will love us and do everything in your power to keep us safe." There was sounds of sniffing and sobbing in the background. She looked at Mary and said, "Will you be my maid of honor?"

"Of course, I will honey. You deserve happiness. John will give you that and so much more."

Without any hesitation, the preacher opened his bible and Mary stood next to Kari's bed. Caleb stood next to John's IV machine. It wasn't exactly the ideal wedding environment, but it was perfect for them. Everyone had pitched in to help it go off without a hitch. Kari was so content. She thought she even felt the baby move and imagined him celebrating too.

They were able to leave the hospital the next day. They had decided to live together at Kari's house. John, Kari, Margaret, and soon a precious baby boy. They were a happy little family. John would sell his home. In all the excitement, John realized that he still had to break the news to his parents. He thought about sending a text, he thought about emailing them, he even considered just writing an old fashioned letter. He didn't want to deal with his opinionated mother. She would never understand. He decided it was time to stop letting her make him feel bad for making his own decisions.

He gave Kari a warning about his mother. She remembered her from the day that she and John first met. She suggested that they invite his parents over for a barbeque so they could break the news to them in person.

John called his mother and slowly began explaining how wild his normally boring life had been in the past few days. Surprisingly, she listened without interrupting him. He may have left out a few details, but asked her if she and his father would come over and meet Kari. His parents agreed.

Sunday came quickly. They had everything ready when John's parents arrived. Kari was glowing. John's mother assumed it was because she was in love. John offered his parents a drink. They all sat outside on the back patio. John listened as his parents got to know Kari better. Sometimes it felt like his mother was almost interrogating her. Somehow she made it seem caring instead of nosey.

She asked Kari where she was born and raised. She asked her about her parents, siblings, work, and pretty much anything else she could think of. Kari realized that John's mother and father would be a part of her life from that day forward. She slowly explained how Mark had passed away. She told them that he made her promise to move on and not stay in mourning for the rest of her life. She told them that she loved Mark and missed him very much. Kari also told them that she never really expected to fall in love again.

John thought he even noticed his mother's eyes glossy with tears at one point while Kari talked. Kari slowly and gently explained how she decided to get pregnant to always have a little piece of Mark with her. John's mom's eyes got really big. Kari told John's parents that she was pregnant and explained how she had to take it easy after the recent surgery. She told them how heroic John was to break the window and rush her to the hospital. If not for John, she and the baby might not have been okay.

John's mom felt so proud of her son. His father smiled with pride too. They probably weren't ready for what Kari and John told them next, but they handled it quite well actually. John told them about the dream and how he knew it was sudden, but he knew Kari was his soulmate and that he couldn't live without her. John's mom felt happy, but also a little jealous that she didn't get to witness her son's nuptials.

After John and Kari were done talking, they all just sat in silence for a few minutes. They could hear someone in the distance mowing their lawn and the sound of a few birds singing. It wasn't really an uncomfortable silence. More like a relief that everything was out in the open.

John's dad was the first to speak, "Well, it sounds like you have both been through a lot in a very short time. Kari, I would like to welcome you to the family. I think being a grandpa could be really fun. I get to spoil my grandson and then send him home so I can still sleep" he chuckled. Who knew that John's dad came over expecting drinks and a steak, but suddenly had so much more. A daughter in-law and soon a grandson.

Next, John's mom spoke, "I am amazed at all you have been through. You are such a strong woman. I admire you. John, I am so proud of the man that you've become. I know I tend to mother you and treat you like a child at times. It's what mom's do. I am very happy for you both. I can see and feel the love between you. I am a little jealous that I didn't get to witness you getting married, but I understand. John has always been the type to go after what he wants. Sometimes he's not patient, but this time I understand why and I think you made an excellent decision."

She stood up and hugged John and Kari and gave them her blessing. Margaret gave a little whimper because she wasn't getting hugged and they all laughed. Dinner was perfect. The food was wonderful. The company was perfect. John's mom and dad told Kari funny stories about when John was younger. They told her about the time that John came home with his knee bleeding. He was limping and had dirt from ear to ear.

His mom assumed he wrecked his bike. John explained that he saw a bird's nest high up in a tree and wanted to get a better look. He climbed up in the tree expecting to see tiny baby birds chirping hungrily. Instead he saw a large, brown breasted bird which he later figured out was the mother.

The bird screeched because John had spooked her and because she was protecting her young. John jumped back because he too had been startled. He missed the first few branches, but scraped his knee on the last few and landed in the dirt. Kari laughed and smiled because she could just picture John trying to be brave as he hobbled home for help.

A few days later, as Kari was resting on the couch per her doctor's orders, the phone rang.

It was John's mom. "I'm just checking on my favorite new daughter in-law."

"I'm doing good, just getting lots of rest for now."

She had been searching online for new pastry ideas for the bakery. She couldn't wait to get back to work, but knew she had to take it easy for now.

"Kari, did anyone happen to take any pictures of the wedding ceremony? I really wish I could have been there, but I understand why John neglected to ask me." Kari could hear sadness in her voice and felt slightly guilty.

"No, nobody thought of that. I'm sorry."

John's mom said she understood. She asked if Kari needed anything. Kari told her that she was just fine and that John would be home early as he only had a few tennis lessons that day. As Kari hung up the phone, she started thinking. She picked up the phone and called Mary. Mary had been calling two or three times a day to check on Kari so when Kari called, Mary was worried.

"Oh no, are you okay? Is the baby okay? Do you need me to bring you something?" Mary sounded like she had switched to coffee instead of tea earlier that morning.

"I'm fine. The baby is fine. I was just talking to John's mom and I have an idea."

Kari called Dr. Wu's office and told him her plan. Dr. Wu made her promise not to overdo it. She was supposed to get as much rest as possible for the next few months. The baby's health depended on it. Mary came over the next day and they waited for John's mom to arrive. They told her that they wanted to her to join them for tea.

When John's mom got there Kari told her that she and John talked it over and they both felt bad that John's mom and dad missed the wedding ceremony. Kari said she got permission from her doctor to plan some light activities. Kari asked John's mom if she would help her and Mary plan another wedding ceremony. She also asked if John's parents would walk her down the aisle. John's mom wasn't an emotional person, but she laughed and cried at the same time out of elation.

"Oh Kari, that would make us so happy, you have no idea how touched I am."

She started talking about flowers, cakes, invitations, and a church then she suddenly stopped and asked how much time she had to plan the ceremony. Kari said she could take as much time as she needed. She had the rest of her life with John so she wasn't in a hurry this time. The three ladies giggled.

Later that day, John arrived home from his lessons. He was in the driveway and he could hear the three women inside laughing and planning another ceremony. He thought about how satisfied he was. He had a family. He was in love. Work was good. He loved life. He walked in and his mother jumped up and ran over to hug him.

"You have made me so happy. I am delighted to plan another ceremony. Thank you so much John."

Then she stepped back and wrinkled up her nose and said, "oh my you're all sweaty, and phew!"

He realized that it was just his mother, that's the way she was and laughed. He hollered out that he would be right back after showering. When he came back downstairs, the women asked him if she liked chocolate cake or white cake. Then they asked him what color of tuxedo he was going to wear. John thought, "wow this was a lot easier at the first ceremony", but he knew how happy he was making Kari and his mom.

The phone rang and it was John's dad, "how are you holding up over there with all the planning?" John's dad almost sounded sarcastic. "I'm wondering what I got myself into" John chuckled.

His dad said he could only imagine. "I'll come pick you up and we'll go grab a burger and a beer and do men stuff", his dad joked.

John was grateful to get out of the house as the women moved on to what type of flowers and music they would use. John asked Kari how she would feel about writing their own vows. She loved the idea and said she would work on it when she got a chance. John kissed her and headed out to lunch with his dad. The menu had so many choices. John was very happy with his life, but realized everything he did lately had so many choices. His dad commented on how happy John was.

It had been a long time since the two of them had some guy time. John settled on a blue cheeseburger and a draft beer. He and his dad talked about cars, weather, sports, and John's dad even said he was considering solar panels for his house. It was fun, just two guys, father and son hanging out.
John's dad looked at his son and smiled, "John, I am so proud of the man that you have become. I don't say it enough, but I love you, son." He patted John on the back.

In that moment John realized just how appreciative he was for all that he had. "I love you too dad."

Later that night after everyone had returned to their homes and much of the planning was coming together. John and Kari were relaxing on the couch. The TV wasn't on and neither of them were talking. They were enjoying the silence. Kari was laying with her head in John's lap staring up at him.

"I hope you know how much I love you" she said softly.

"I do" he replied and "I hope you know that I love you too."

He leaned down and kissed her slowly and softly. Her skin was so smooth and he stroked her cheek. He turned on the stereo and changed it to the soft rock channel. She sat up and he held out his hand and asked her to dance. There in the living room, he held her close and they swayed to the music. Air Supply was singing about being lost in love and that described exactly how they felt, lost in love.

The next day was Saturday, John got up early and made breakfast. He delivered it to Kari with a glass of orange juice, a single red rose, and a small neatly wrapped package.

"What is this" she asked as she rubbed her eyes.

"It's breakfast in bed for my wife"

She drank some juice and ate a piece of bacon and then picked up the package. The wrapping paper had little ABC blocks on it and all the letters were blue. She unwrapped it. It was a paperback book of baby names.

"I thought we could start thinking of a name for our son"

Although John had never said that before, it had a nice ring to it, "our son". They started flipping through the book. They laughed at some of the outdated names in the book. Some of the names neither of them had ever heard, for example Wadsworth, Thaddeus, or Winston. Then there were names that they didn't like because of what they were associated with. They both kind of liked the name Jason, but John remembered the weird kid in grade school that ate paste was named Jason.

Kari felt the same way about Josh. She went to school with a boy named Josh who was a big bully. They decided to write down five of each of their favorites and go from there. Kari picked Cody, Jackson, Lucas, Craig, and Stephen. John showed Kari his list. He wrote down Zach, Cory, Brandon, Frederick, and Markus. As soon as Kari saw the name Markus, she knew that was it. John felt it was a way to honor the baby's biological father and Kari's late husband.

They had so much to do. They had to help with the wedding ceremony which growing more and more detailed by the day. Put the nursery together. Sell John's house. It was exhausting. Along with Mary and John's parents, they all decided on a date. May 22nd sounded perfect for the wedding. It was a right around the corner. They would have time to mail out invitations.

Kari was thinking maybe 40 invitations while John's mom was thinking more like 140. Kari just gave in and let her plan away besides she was really enjoying planning the ceremony for John and Kari and it was helping them bond. One afternoon John's phone rang.

"I'm calling about the house you have for sale" a woman's voice said. "Yes, what questions can I answer about it for you?" John replied. "Well, what can you tell me about it?"

John thought the woman's voice sounded familiar, but couldn't quite place it.

"It is a two-bedroom townhouse. It has all new appliances. I just repainted inside. There is a two car garage. I'm not sure if you have children, but it's close to the elementary school."

John was trying to remember all the top selling points from when he purchased the house years ago.

"When can I meet you there to look at it?"

The woman asked as if she didn't care about anything John had just told her.

"Oh, pretty much anytime. Just let me know and I'll schedule a time to show it to you. If I am not available, my wife can meet you there."

There was silence on the other end.

"Hello?" John thought maybe he hung up on the woman. He checked the phone, it still said connected.

"I'm here" the woman said coldly. John thought that was really odd. "Will you be available tomorrow afternoon, John?" He didn't remember telling the woman his name, but he didn't think much of it.

"Yes, I can meet you there at 4. How does that sound?"

"Fine, see you tomorrow at 4, John," the woman said coldly.

"I'm sorry, I didn't catch your name" he said.

"It's JJ."

John hung up the phone excited at the possibility of selling his home. It hadn't been on the market for very long. John felt a slight pit in his stomach. Maybe it was that the home he was selling had been his bachelor pad. He could do whatever he wanted. He was in charge of what he watched and what he ate. The only person he answered to there was Margret.

Then he remembered how lonely he was. Nobody to talk to or laugh with. He was so thankful for his new life. His life with his new wife and son, and of course Margret. John walked into the living room and told Kari that he had someone interested in the house. He told her that after work the next day he had to meet a potential buyer at the house at 4.

The next day at work seemed to fly by. Before John knew it the clock said 3:30. He showered at the club and headed down the familiar route to his old house. He lived close but thought he should get there early. He pulled into the driveway and opened the garage door with the electric opener in this car. He almost pulled into the garage, but thought he better leave his car in the driveway so he could show how spacious the garage was.

Another selling point that he liked when he bought the home. He went inside and opened up the windows to let some fresh air in since he hadn't been there in a while. He was in the bedroom and he heard a car pull up in the driveway. He went to the front door and opened it up to welcome his guest. John couldn't believe his eyes. JJ, John realized quickly was also known as Jaycee. There she stood in the doorway. John thought, no way could this be happening. Everything in his life was so perfect and here she was trying to ruin it.

"Jaycee, what are you doing here?"

"Oh hello love, I'm here to look at your house" she tilted her head slightly and smiled at John. "I told you we do crazy things when we're in love"

"Jaycee, I'm not now nor have I ever been in love with you. I am married and I'm about to be a father"

"Are you kidding me, John?" Jaycee screamed.

John realized how delusional she really was. Jaycee made it seem like they had dated for years and John betrayed her. He just stared at her in silence. He didn't even know what to say to her. She is beyond crazy he thought to himself.
Jaycee whirled around and grabbed the mini blinds in the living room and screamed at the top of her lungs, "I will not let that tramp steal my man. You belong to me John! Me not her!"

She tore the blinds off the window and threw them at him. Next she went into the kitchen and picked up the table and threw it against the sliding glass door shattering it. Jaycee kicked the stove, ripped the key holder off the wall and it slammed to the ground. Next, she reached for the towel rack. She yanked it off the wall with force and stood there with the sharp metal rod in her hand and glared at John. She started to come after him with it raised in the air.

Instead of running from her which he thought is what she probably wanted he stepped into her space and reached for what had once held a small kitchen towel with a rooster on it, but was now being swung violently at this head. He lunged at her to grab the weapon away but missed.

She stepped back and swung it at John. He felt pain in his head and something warm on his face. He wiped his hand across his face and saw blood. A lot of blood. He realized from the floor that the front door was still open. He began to yell for help. Jaycee looked at him and laughed, "Nobody is going to hear you John."

Everything went gray and fuzzy then black. He felt someone licking his face. He opened his eyes to see Mitzi, Caleb's dog. He slowly turned to the left and saw Caleb standing next to a police officer. John couldn't make out what they were saying and he couldn't believe how bad his head hurt. He looked to the right and another office had Jaycee in handcuffs. She was crying and trying to put on a show like she didn't know what was happening.

He couldn't hear what she was saying either other than, "I have no idea, when I got here the door was open and he was lying on the floor. I can't imagine what happened to him." He wanted to yell that she was crazy and lying, but just like in the dream he had before, he opened his mouth but nothing would come out.

"John, don't try to talk" Caleb said as he kneeled down next to John. "You're going to be fine. The ambulance is on the way."

John thought why would he need an ambulance, he was so confused and his head was pounding. He heard the roar of the siren and felt too weak to fight staying awake.

John woke up to the sounds of beeping machines and nurses talking. He thought he was dreaming. He felt scared. He tried to figure out what was happening to him. The nurse looked at him with sadness. He heard the doctor say, "nurse, give him a shot of Valium, he's waking up and he's in shock"

Chapter 2

Kari, Mary, and John's mom had just finished their tea. They felt good about the plans they made for the wedding ceremony. Kari was tired, she was definitely starting to feel pregnant. Kari heard a car pull up and assumed John was back from showing the house. The doorbell rang and Mary jumped up to see who it was. It was Caleb. Kari was going to tell him that John wasn't back yet. Caleb looked awful. His eyes were deep red and his hair was a mess. He looked like he hadn't slept in days.

"Caleb, are you alright?" Kari asked

"I'm fine Kari." Caleb said, as his voice almost sounded like it was quivering.

"I was taking Mitzi out for a walk. We were walking past John's old house. I remembered him saying that he was showing the house to a potential buyer. As we got closer, I heard a loud commotion and yelling."

Caleb took just a second to catch his breath, he knew he was talking fast, but he had so much to try to get out in a short time. "I started to go into the house and I heard John yelling for help." Caleb seen all of the color drain from Kari's face, but he had to keep going.

"There was a woman hitting him with a sharp metal rod. I grabbed it out of her hands and shoved her away from John. I called 911 on my cell phone. I realized as I was on the phone that woman was Jaycee."

It didn't matter what Caleb said after that, Kari felt her throat tighten and tasted an awful taste like bile. She stood up but felt dizzy. Mary grabbed her arm and sat her back down. John's mom asked if John was ok and where he was.

The hospital wasn't very far from Kari's house. It was one of the things that gave her comfort. She knew when she went into labor she could get to the hospital in a matter of minutes.

John's mom was terrified, but she didn't want to let Kari know how worried she was. Kari was supposed to be relaxing for her health and the health of the baby.

John had always been one of those kids who made his mom worry. When he was 10, he loved to read comic books. John decided he had super powers and tried to fly off the roof of his father's garage. It didn't work like he thought it would and he ended up with several broken bones.

When John was in high school, he convinced his father to let him buy a motorcycle. John's mom didn't like to think about him riding that thing. One afternoon on her commute home, she was stuck in traffic. In her rear-view mirror she noticed something moving quickly in and out of the cars. Her heart just about stopped when she noticed it was a blue Suzuki GSX-R. The rider had a shiny, electric blue helmet.

It was John. She thought to herself, there was no way that could be her son riding so carelessly. When he got next to her car, he honked and waved at his mother. She felt sick, scared, and angry all at once. When she got home, she told his father. She heard them later in the garage laughing about how paranoid she was.

The nurse led them to the waiting room. None of them spoke. They were all very concerned as none of them knew John's status. They had been sitting in the waiting room for about ten minutes. An older gentleman with snow white hair came in and asked if they were there about John. The doctor explained that John had a concussion.

He went on to explain that were basically three types of concussions. Grade 1 was mild, no loss of consciousness. Grade 2 was moderate which obviously meant that is was a stronger version of Grade 1. Then he said there was Grade 3, a severe concussion which usually caused some type of amnesia. When Kari heard that she felt her thoughts begin to race. She thought that if John had amnesia and didn't remember her, she was going to have to start all over again. The nerves were just starting to spin out of control when she heard the doctor say, "thankfully, it's between a grade 2 and 3. John is not showing any signs of amnesia. He is asking to see Kari."

They all turned to look at Kari. She tried to smile bravely.

She followed the doctor down the hall. It seemed like it was taking them forever to get to John's room. She wanted to run to him. She wanted him to know that she was there for him and always would be. Kari wasn't quite prepared for how rough John looked.

His head was wrapped in miles of white gauze. His right eye was a plum like shade of purple and almost swollen shut. His cheek had stiches. He saw her and his face lit up and he smiled at her with pure love in his eyes. The doctor pulled a big mauve colored chair up next to the bed and she sat next to John and picked up his hand and kissed it. She loved him so dearly.

"Well, how did showing the house go?" she tried to lighten the mood
John smirked and said, "You know, it could have gone better"
Kari said, "We don't have to talk about it now. Please just rest. I'll be right here by your side" she held his hand on his cheek for several minutes.

John's mom, Caleb, and Mary were allowed in the room. None of them knew what to say so they just made small talk. John's mom commented on the color scheme of the walls and asked if he was comfortable. Mary stood by the window and commented on the view. Caleb tried to bring up the basketball game that was coming up on the sports channel.

Chapter 3

John was able to return home the next day. Since both Kari and John had strict orders to take it easy, they watched a lot of movies, played board games, and ordered pizza for the next several days. John had placed a temporary order of protection against Jaycee. She was not allowed to come within 1500 feet of himself or Kari.

John knew it was really just a piece of paper, but hoped that the threat of jail was enough to keep her from breaking the rules. Mary would call each day and drop off treats every now and then. Caleb stopped by to see if they needed anything. John's parents did anything they could to help.

One morning, John heard what sounded like a semi outside. He looked out the window and saw a U Haul truck backing up to the house next door. He didn't know the neighbors well at all. He probably would have gone over to see if they needed help, but he was still moving slow. The man driving the truck noticed John watching him and waved and smiled. John waved back like a good neighbor. John made his way back to the couch.

He couldn't remember ever being so bored. At least he was in good company. John and Kari decided to find a small project to occupy them while they were healing. They decided to work on the nursery for baby Markus. They went to the store and gathered up paint swatches. They shopped for furniture and read books on how to get prepared. As the day grew closer they became more and more excited.

John's parents called one afternoon and invited he and Kari over for dinner. They agreed. John's parents house was looking like it could use a remodel. They had purchased it when John was in elementary school. When they got to his parents' house, they talked about how John and Kari were feeling. They were both feeling great and their lives were starting to get back to normal. They cherished the days without drama.

John's dad asked John about the neighborhood that he and Kari lived in. John told him that it was a nice little neighborhood. There was a coffee and ice cream shop within walking distance. He said all the neighbors kind of just kept to themselves. John also mentioned that the people next door had to moved to another state and their house sold right away so they would be getting new neighbors any day.

John's mom said, "New neighbors, that will be exciting."

"As long as they are the nosey kind" John laughed.

"Do you think that people consider us nosey neighbors?" John's dad asked.

"No, what kind of question is that?" John was confused.

"We just want to make sure that you'll welcome us to the neighborhood since we are going to be living next door" John's mom announced and then stood back and waited for John and Kari to process what she had just told them.

It took a minute, but then John said, "wait, are you telling me that you bought the house next door to us?"

"Yes we are neighbor!"

John looked at Kari whose eyes were huge and she sat there speechless.

John's mom said, "We know that you could use some extra help every now and then. We want to be close enough to be there whenever you need us. We probably should have asked first, but we were feeling spontaneous."

John's parents told he and Kari that they were going to start moving in later that month and that they were going to put their house on the market immediately.

"Be careful who you meet to show the house to" John said halfway joking.

Dinner was wonderful and they all enjoyed themselves. At first Kari wasn't sure how it would be having them right next door, but she did enjoy their company and it would be nice for a first time mother to have help so close. Kari started thinking how funny it would be if

Mary and Rod moved in on the other side and Caleb and Mitzi could live next to them. Then she thought to herself how drastically her life had changed in such a short time and how happy she was. She felt loved and appreciated. They were barely buckled up and headed home when John started laughing and shaking his head

"I guess we're going to have new neighbors" he said it like he almost couldn't believe it. He still wasn't sure how he felt about the shocker that he just heard.

Kari rubbed his back and smiled at him before she spoke, "I've really gotten close to your mother. I love your father too. I am happy that they will be closer. It will be great having help close by. I think it will be good for all of us."

John said, "who are you trying to convince here, me or yourself?" and they laughed.

When they got home as they pulled up, Kari found herself thinking of the house that was vacant next door. She could imagine Christmas and Thanksgiving together. She could picture John's dad playing tag with Markus. She had so much to look forward to.

John and Mary's husband Rod had become good friends. When John got home he called Rod to tell him about his parent's announcement. Next he called Caleb to tell him. After talking to them and having a little time to think about it he decided that maybe it would be nice. After all, he could see that it made Kari almost blissful.

John and Kari had looked through about a hundred colors and types of paint. They had researched what type of paint would be safest. They learned that most paints contained something called VOC which stands for volatile organic compound. It is found in things like gasoline, colored markers, and mothballs for example. Sounded horrible. They finally found a VOC free paint in a shade called Seaside. They found little wall clings of sailboats, starfish, and other ocean themed objects.

Kari liked shopping online. It made it a lot easier on her. She found pretty much everything on her nursery checklist. She found a crib, blankets, bedding, diapering supplies, a baby monitor, and a smoke and carbon monoxide detector. She had hired someone to help run the bakery for now so she was trying to find stuff to do. The book she was reading called it nesting.
John had just finished the crib and his parent's called and asked if they could stop by. They brought a gift with them. John's grandpa was an artist and a woodworker.

He had handmade the most gorgeous rocking chair for John's mom when she was pregnant with him. It was made out of walnut and maple. He had carved tiny carousel horses and hearts very delicately into the wood. Kari could tell that it must have taken hours and days to make it. It was so exquisite. The hormones combined with the generosity of such a heartfelt gift brought her to tears. She thanked John's parents through her waterworks and hugged them tightly.

Everything was coming together just as planned. The wedding ceremony and John's parents move were both coming right up. Kari sat back in the rocking chair and closed her eyes all while wearing the biggest smile she could to show her level of content.

Chapter 4

It was very early on a Saturday morning when John's parents started moving in next door. They had hired movers to load and unload everything to make it easier on themselves and everyone else. Dr. Wu had given Kari permission to help with the unpacking as long as she didn't lift anything heavy or overdo it. The baby was developing just fine and Kari was looking more and more pregnant each day. John and his dad worked on unpacking the garage and Kari and John's mom worked at unpacking inside the house. Unpacking made her remember when she and Mark bought the house next door.

Before buying the house, they lived in an apartment building on the second floor. Kari was so thankful that she didn't have to climb those steps anymore, especially now. They used to laugh about the old lady next door to them who always had several boxes of cat food delivered, but didn't have any cats. Then there was the little girl on the other side of them who lived with her parents. Every Time they went out, the little girl would open the door just a tiny bit and watch them. When they would try to say hello or make eye contact with her, she would slam the door shut really fast and Kari and Mark would laugh every time because it was so strange.

She loved her house, but after Mark died she just felt lonely and sad. That's why she spent so much time at the bakery. She didn't have to feel lonely or sad anymore.

John's mom watched Kari as she seemed to be in a totally different place. She took a moment to really look at Kari. She had such beautiful big eyes with really long lashes. She was beautiful in her own unique way. John's mom could certainly see how happy Kari and John were together. She felt like Kari had a big heart and loved helping people. John was the same way. She thought to herself that John and Kari were made for each other. Things have a funny way of working themselves out.

Kari looked up suddenly and saw John's mom watching her. She smiled and said, "oh sorry, I think you caught me reminiscing."

"Penny for your thoughts?" John's mom said.

"I was just remembering when Mark and I moved into the house next door. I thought we would live there together forever, but God had a different plan for Mark. I do miss him. He was my first true love, but obviously not my last."

Kari stopped and wiped a tear from her eye. "I guess being pregnant comes with a lot of emotions that I never even knew that I had" both women laughed.

John's mom was quiet for a few seconds and then slowly said, "I remember both times that I was pregnant. I was a mess. I cried all the time. I was always starving and then...." she just stopped mid sentence.

She looked up shocked and said, "I can't believe I was just talking about that. I've never told anyone except John's father. I was pregnant after John. They called it hyperthyroidism, they said that my thyroid produces too many hormones that interfered with my levels of estrogen. We were on the way to surprise our parents and tell them I was pregnant. We stopped at a rest area. I went in to go to the bathroom and my underwear were bloody. I ran back out and we headed for the nearest town with a hospital. By the time we got there, it was too late. I lost the baby. We didn't finish our trip, we headed home and I cried all the way back" as she finished telling Kari, both of them were in tears. Through sadness and loss, they had a bonding moment that neither of them would forget.

The two women were hugging and sniffling when John and his father came in for a break. They could tell right away that something had just happened.

John said, "is everything alright?"

Kari said, "we're just having a moment" she tried to shrug it off as it wasn't her place to repeat what John's mom had just told her.

"John, please sit down" his mom said, "there's something I have never told you about."

John's dad shook his head and looked sad, "Oh no, you're not going to tell me that I was adopted are you?" John often used humor to get out of uncomfortable situations.

"No, John you're not adopted" his mom laughed. She picked up his hand and slowly recanted the story that she had just finished telling Kari.

"Mom, I am so sorry. I had no idea that you had to go through something so emotionally and physically painful" John held him mom close and hugged her as she cried.

The sound of the doorbell interrupted the uncomfortable silence. It was Mary. She had brought over fresh cupcakes from Kari's bakery. Mary stopped by to make sure things at the bakery were running smoothly. She decided to bring cupcakes by to give everyone a nice treat and a much deserved break. Mary noticed an odd vibe in the room, but didn't acknowledge it. Instead she insisted on everyone having a cupcake. They were red velvet with cream cheese frosting.

Mary stayed to help and they all worked together unpacking John's parents. John's mom was thinking how nice it was to have so much help. After all, she did have the wedding ceremony coming right up. Thinking about everything she still had to do was exhausting. She wondered why she always took on so much. She decided that it was that she liked to stay busy so she didn't have so much time to think. The rest of the day flew by. Caleb stopped by to help and Rod did too. They knew they would all sleep good that night. The majority of the unpacking was done so they ordered pizza and ate together as one big happy family.

Chapter 5

John's parents had lived in their new house for a few days and were starting to get used to everything. John's mom sat down at the kitchen table with her list and supplies. She had several people who had rsvp'd and she wrote each of their names on a place card for the reception. She sat all of those in a pile on the right side of the table. Next she took out the cameras. She bought 20 disposable cameras and planned to place them on the tables at the reception so other people could take pictures and then she would send them in to be developed.

She wondered if in this day and age that anyone ever sent film away to be developed. She felt old. She placed the cameras in a box with a lid and marked the top of the lid "cameras" and put it on the left side of the table. She continued this routine with all of her supplies and lists one by one. There was a pile for flowers, catering, the cake, the music, and more. She was enjoying herself, but it was a lot of work so she would have Kari over to help as often as possible. The two of them had become very close. Wedding gifts started arriving. There was so much excitement in the air.

John and Kari had decided to write their own vows. It was raining and gloomy outside so Kari made some tea and grabbed her favorite blanket and sat on the couch. She took out a notebook and started to scribble some ideas down. She had a good idea what she wanted to say, but wrote things down that she wanted to make sure to incorporate.

She started to write and she felt Markus start moving around. He gave her a healthy kick which made her laugh out loud. Then she felt the strangest thing. It was like a little jump every few seconds in her belly. At first she was stumped and growing concerned, but then she remembered reading about it. Markus had the hiccups. She drank some water and they went away quickly. As she began to write it was like the pen knew what she wanted to say, it practically danced across the blank paper.

My dearest John,
Not too long ago, I was in a bad place. A sad place. My husband, Mark passed away very suddenly. It blindsided me. I didn't know

how to go on. I was broken. I decided that I wanted to carry on his personality and kindness. I wanted to create a little piece of him. Through technology, I was able to get pregnant. I didn't plan on meeting you and falling in love, but that's just what happened. We did have some miscommunication and a rough patch, but what's meant to be always finds it way. The definition of a soul mate is a person ideally suited for another as a close friend or romantic partner. You are both of those things to me and so much more. I could never imagine my life without you. Thank you for choosing me as your wife.

She read it twice and decided it was perfect. There was so much more that she could say, but she always regretting going to those wedding ceremonies that last hours. Besides she had the rest of their lives to show and tell John how she felt and she was looking forward to it.

John had a tennis lesson to give that day, but the child he was teaching was ill so the lesson had to be cancelled. It was a beautiful day. He decided to walk over to the park across the street to work on his vows. He put his stuff in his car. He kept a notebook in his car for writing down things to work on for the people who he taught lessons to. He kicked his shoes off and sat down in the soft, cushiony grass. He closed his eyes and thought about his wife. He had never loved anyone the way he loved her and he had almost screwed that up. He opened the notebook. He didn't know how to start. He thought about it and decided on:

Kari, my beautiful bride,
For a long time, the only woman that could put up with me everyday had four legs, a tail, and really bad breath. Being your husband has taught me love, appreciation and a kind of happiness that I wasn't sure existed. You told me that you could never thank me enough for rescuing you, but in reality you rescued me. You are so kind and willing to help anyone. You love so deeply. The night we made pizza and stayed up all night talking, I knew you were the one. Thank you for being my wife. Thank you for showing me that love is real.

He read it through all the scribbled out things he thought sounded too cheesy. He loved it because described how he felt about his wife. He put his stuff in his backpack and laid down. He was on his back watching the clouds float by. When he was younger, he loved lying in the grass and making shapes out of the clouds. He heard the sound of the ice cream truck and children screaming as they raced each other to see who would get their tasty treat first.

He loved orange creamsicles, but he had not had one in years. He sat up and saw that the line was about 12 kids and a mom pushing a stroller with an impatient toddler unhappy that it wasn't his turn. John slipped his shoes on and casually strolled over to get his orange creamsicle. It was just as he remembered it. Cold, creamy, and satisfying.

When John got home, Kari was baking cookies. When he was a kid those were his favorite two snacks, chocolate chip cookies, and creamsicles. To think he was going to get both of his favorites treats in the same day was wonderful. He kissed his wife and asked when the cookies would be ready to eat.

"Not all of them are for you mister." she said, "Your mom isn't feeling well, so I'm taking most of them to her."

"She doesn't even like cookies, I'll just eat them for her" John joked.

Then on a serious note he asked, "What's wrong with mom?" as he snuck a cookie off the tray.

"Just between you and I, I think she has worn herself out with all this planning for the wedding ceremony and reception. Don't get me wrong, I appreciate everything she's doing and I try to help out as much as I can. She's overdoing it. I thought I would take over some cookies and milk and let her proofread my vows. I finished them today." she was beaming with pride.

Her vows were perfect and the cookies were too. She watched as John ate his third one. She laughed and kissed him and said she would be next door. Kari's belly was getting so big she could almost balance the plate of cookies on it she thought as she chuckled. She knocked and then walked in as she always did. John's mom had her feet kicked up sitting in the recliner and she started to get up.

"No, no please don't get up. I brought you a few things." Kari smiled.

"Oh really, why?" John's mom asked jokingly.

"You have been overdoing it with all this planning. I wanted you to rest and enjoy some cookies and milk. I rescued these ones before your son got to them. I also brought cold milk."

Then she opened the bag and grabbed an envelope. She handed it to John's mom and asked her if she minded proofreading the vows that Kari wrote.

"I would be honored" John's mom said. She sat up in her chair and started reading. Before she was done, she grabbed a tissue from the end table. She wiped her eyes and told Kari that it was perfect.

"Thank you for asking me to read them. I'm so happy that you came into our lives Kari. You have made all of us so happy."

After a few minutes Kari returned home. Before she left, she made John's mom promise to stop working so much and take it easy. When she got home, she found John lying on the couch holding his stomach.

"What's wrong?" Kari asked.

"I don't feel good" John said quietly.

Kari looked over at the stove to see that John had eaten all of the remaining cookies. She just shook her head and laughed.

"Did you seriously eat all of those cookies John?"

"I did and before I got home, I had an orange creamsicle from the ice cream truck" John groaned "I'm going to get off this couch and go check on mom. How is she?"

Kari said "she's just tired, but I made her promise to slow down."

John very slowly sat up and waddled out the door as if he were the pregnant one. Kari couldn't help but to smile at him and headed off to check on his mom.
John knocked and then went in. By then, both of his parents were home. They were sitting in their recliners eating cookies and watching TV. John winced at the sight of more cookies. He sat down and asked how his mom was. John's dad said that if she wasn't feeling better in the

next couple of days, her doctor wanted her to get a check up.

"I'm fine, I'm just getting old" John's mom joked.

"Well since you're both here, maybe I could read my vows out loud and you could give me your constructive feedback" he looked at his parents for their answer although he already knew they would be delighted to hear what he wrote.

When he finished reading, both of his parents looked proud and happy that he was their son. They congratulated him and thanked him for letting them be a part of it. His mom even said she was feeling better. John hugged his parents and went back home to his wife.

John's mom went in later that week to see her doctor. They gave her a stress test to check her heart. He also prescribed some anxiety medication to her and told her to slow down so she didn't put herself at risk for a heart attack. He told her to stay calm and eat healthy.

A friend of the family was a wedding planner so she offered to take over planning the ceremony which seemed to get more and more detailed. John and Kari found it kind of silly since they were already married, but went along with it because they wanted to make his mom happy. John's mom even planned a rehearsal dinner. It was going to be at a restaurant called La Famille which meant family in French. The rehearsal dinner was the following night. At first everyone was anxious and could hardly wait for the night to arrive. Later looking back, they wished it would have ended a lot better than it did.

Chapter 6

The day of the rehearsal dinner started off rough. John overslept and was running late for his first tennis lesson of the day. It was usually a quick trip to the club, but that day it seemed to take him forever to get there. Kari had a meeting with a client who wanted to talk to her about buying the bakery. She loved the bakery, but with Markus arriving very soon, she didn't know how she could divide her time fairly. John's parents had to pick up their clothes from the dry cleaners and get their hair cut. Everyone had something to do.

John got ready to head home. When he got to his car, there were several pieces of notebook paper stuck to the windows of his car. On each page it said "7:00P.M. rehearsal dinner at La Famille. See you there" John thought it was his mom's subtle way of reminding him. He wondered why she didn't just stop by the tennis court like she usually did. Then he remembered that she had not quite been acting like herself.

He ran home, took a shower and picked up Kari who looked stunning with her pregnancy glow and a sapphire blue dress that matched her eyes almost perfectly. As they drove to the restaurant they talked about how happy they would be when this was all over and everything could return to normal.

Everyone close to John and Kari were there. They were all enjoying their food and chit chatting about life. John happened to look over at his mom. She had always been there for him when he needed her. He was lucky to have her for a mom.

He mouthed the words "I love you" to her.

She smiled and mouthed it right back to him. He was smiling at her when he watched her face turn a pale shade of white. She grabbed her chest and said "please help me" then she fell forward.

Champagne spilled across the table and the glass broke. John's dad and John both ran to her side. Mary jumped into action and called 911. The ambulance arrived in about 5 minutes although John was sure it felt more like 25 min. His mother sat slouched in the chair that she had just been celebrating in. Now she was celebrating, she wasn't moving at all. John felt helpless.

Here was the woman who kissed his boo boos when he got hurt at a little boy. The woman who drove him to the ER when he thought he could fly off of this dad's garage roof. The woman who was always there for him no matter what. Anytime he needed help there she was, right next to his side helping him. Now that it was his turn he couldn't do anything but wait for the E.M.T's.

The hospital smelled like bleach and old stale coffee. There was a chill in the waiting room. It was certainly not warm enough outside for them to have the air conditioning on. John's dad came into the waiting room. They could see he had been crying. John's dad was a strong, prideful man. At that moment though, he just looked defeated. He told John and Kari that John's mom wanted to talk to them. Of course they headed to the room she was in. The doctor was walking out and said to keep it short. John sat on one side of her and Kari sat on the other side. She held their hands and spoke slowly in a sore, raspy voice that John hardly even recognized.

"Thank you both for reading the beautiful vows that you wrote to each other to me." She had to stop catch her breath.

She swallowed hard and said, "I hope you know how happy I am for both of you. True love is hard to find these days. Please cherish each other and that precious baby."

John started to cry, "Mom why are you talking like this? You're going to be at the ceremony, we're just going to postpone it until you're feeling better."

Kari nodded and said "Of course we will wait for you.
John's mom smiled and closed her eyes and said, "I'm sorry you two, but I don't think I'm going to make it."

www.ingramcontent.com/pod-product-compliance
Lightning Source LLC
LaVergne TN
LVHW041634070526
838199LV00052B/3353